MURDERERS!

A story of Burke and Hare

by

Karen Doherty

rooshie doo

Published by Gallus Publications,
PO Box 29055,
Dunfermline KY11 4YL

Cover design by Liam Doherty, with original artwork by Aimee Brown of St. Paul's Primary School, Glenrothes (front cover) and Dale Cuthbertson of Commercial Primary School, Dunfermline (back cover). Illustrations by Frank McCormick.

ISBN 0-9546625-2-0

A catalogue record for this book is available from the British Library.

Printed and bound by Printing Services (Scotland) Ltd., Broomhead Drive, Dunfermline.

Author's acknowledgements

I would like to thank the staff of Edinburgh City Libraries for their assistance in the research for this book; and also Owen Dudley Edwards for his book 'Burke and Hare'.

This story is dedicated to the Doherty men.

Karen Doherty, Kirkcaldy, July 2004

CHAPTER ONE

Crouched motionless in the shadows, Calum held his breath. The last tray of pies had been delivered to the hotel. It was now or never. A rat was already furtively scuttling towards the cart. If Calum got it right he could 'gather' a pie while the cook was paying the deliveryman. He watched the rat, took careful aim and threw the stone as hard as he could. The But the rat was smart, saw it coming and darted off with the pie crust before Calum could move.

    He swore under his breath as he stood up from behind the barrel. He'd had his eye on that crust since early morning, as soon as it had fallen from the baker's tray; but had had to wait until the coast was clear. At that time it was still warm and delicious. By now it was a bit scuffed and soggy looking; but still…

This way of foraging for food did have its risks though. Last time he'd tried to 'gather' a pie the baker had caught him, and beaten him with a butter pat till his skin was black and blue. Calum didn't want to go through that again. Sadly, this time round, his pie crust and the rat were both long gone.

Calum was starving. He hadn't eaten anything for two days. Living on the streets of Edinburgh was hard. He was used to being alone although he often dreamt of his mother. Sometimes he woke up crying. It was times

like this that he missed her most. Had it really been three years since she died? He had hoped that 1829 was going to be his lucky year but so far things seemed no different. Still, it was only March. Maybe when the warmer months came in, his luck would change.

Calum hated wintertime. Lots of beggars died during the winter months, huddled in doorways and under bridges. He used to lie with the beggars for heat, but most of them would steal from you as soon as look at you. They even stole the scarf his mother knitted just before she died. Calum was proud that he was no beggar. His mother would have hated that. He always worked to earn a penny or if he couldn't work he'd 'gather' what was dropped or left lying around.

Sighing, Calum wrapped his piece of sacking around him and headed off, in the deepening dusk, towards the alehouse. At least his boots kept his feet *almost* dry. With any luck he might be able to run a few errands for a drayman. Maybe Calum could be a drayman like Big Davie when he grew up. Davie had let Calum ride with him to deliver the barrels to the alehouses. Once he even got to hold the reins. How he loved the big Clydesdales. They were magnificent horses. Proud, strong and reliable.

Suddenly Calum heard a creaking noise to his left. He sidled into a close mouth, and stood perfectly still. He had learned long ago that being eleven, and alone, was often risky. He was taking no chances. His breath hung in the cold March air, visible even in the moonlight. Calum could feel hairs on his neck rising and his eyes strained to make sense of the shapes in the shadows. Pressing his back against the damp wall he peered round the corner of the close, as two men struggled to move a wheelbarrow across

the uneven cobbles. Whatever they had in the barrow was
very heavy, because their breath came in grunting gasps
as they heaved and shoved. For a second Calum wondered
if it was worth his while following them – perhaps they
had some tatties in the barrow? Calum's mouth watered
at the thought of a tattie roasted on a workman's brazier.
Hundreds of Irishmen were in the city after finishing the
Union Canal and many could be found huddled round
braziers drinking and roaring, rambling on about 'the Ould
Country'. Calum reckoned it couldn't be that great if they
stayed in freezing Auld Reekie instead of heading home

to the land they claimed to love.

A rat scuttled across Calum's foot and he jerked it off in disgust. The rat screeched and ran off. Immediately the two men whirled round, the barrow forgotten.

Calum froze. One of the men stepped forward, peering into the darkness. The blade of a knife glinted from his fist. Calum held his breath and pressed harder against the wall. The man edged a little closer.

'There's something moving over there.'

'It's a rat ...come on. There's seven pounds an' ten shillings waiting for us.'

'I'm sure I saw someone but.'

'Ah, no. Who'd be out at this time of night but the Resurrectionists? And they only go for the dead - so we'll be fine.' Calum realised they were both Irishmen. The two men laughed softly and made their way off into the shadows again.

Calum had heard of Resurrectionists. Mrs. Murdoch said they were evil people who went to graveyards and stole bodies to sell to doctors. Why were the men laughing? What was funny about stealing bodies?

Calum relaxed and slid down the wall a little. His heart was thumping so hard he felt sure they'd hear it. He shivered and wrapped his sacking tightly about him until his breathing returned to normal. Looking round once more to check they'd gone, he sprinted all the way to the alehouse as fast as he could, splashing through puddles as he ran. With any luck Calum could sneak into the drayman's stable. It would be warm and dry and safe. Tonight especially, the city seemed even darker than normal.

CHAPTER TWO

Calum rubbed his eyes and stretched out his cramped legs. Stables were grand places to keep warm for the night but sharing a stall with a shire horse meant there wasn't much room. Picking a stray piece of straw from his cheek, Calum sat up and yawned. It was still dark but he knew it was morning. He could hear Jamie preparing the feedbags for the horses as usual and whistling to himself as he worked.

'Hiya Jamie!' said Calum, getting to his feet. 'You're cheery this mornin.'

' Ooh mercy!' yelped Jamie, dropping the oat scoop. 'I didnae see ye there Calum. What a fricht ye gave me.'

'Sorry Jamie. Do ye want a hand tae feed the horses?'

' Em… aye…ta Calum. You see tae Cora and I'll do the big fella. C'mon by, Samson.'

Jamie was nineteen but acted much younger. He didn't understand a lot of things but his heart was as big as Arthur's Seat. Sometimes Calum felt like Jamie was his little brother. Calum didn't like it when people called him Daft Jamie, but Jamie just laughed and told him not to worry.

After Calum's mum had died there had been nowhere for him to go. No-one else to care for him. The city was full of workers and travellers but none interested in a small, motherless boy. Jamie had been the first person to show him kindness. He shared his food, brought him some milk and gave him a blanket. Calum owed him a lot.

'There's a wee bittie bread and some cheese in ma pouch Calum if you're hungry…' said Jamie, opening his little snuff box.

Calum couldn't understand why anybody would want to take snuff. He'd tried it once just to please Jamie but it made him sneeze and his eyes water.

'Aye, a wee bit Jamie. Ta.' said Calum, trying not to drool as he opened the pouch. The bread smelt so good and as for the cheese… it had been a long time since he'd eaten some cheese.

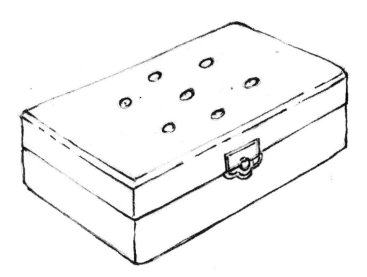

Having seen to the animals, Calum sat down beside Jamie and chewed on his breakfast. He loved to watch Jamie use his tiny copper spoon to lift out some snuff. Jamie didn't need much to make him happy but oh, how he loved his snuffbox. He called it his days of the week because it had seven holes in the lid. It glinted in the lantern light.

The tiny flash reminded Calum of the knife blade and he shuddered. Jamie looked over at him, puzzled.

'Are ye cauld Calum? Ye can wear ma jaiket if ye like...' said Jamie starting to rise, his face troubled.

'No, it's all right Jamie. I'm no' cauld. I was just rememberin' somethin' I saw last night.'

'How? Was it a ghostie Calum? I get scared o' ghosties tae.'

Calum smiled to himself. 'Naw Jamie, it wasn't a ghostie. It was twa men, hurlin' a barra.'

'That's no' scary Calum. I hurl a barra for Mr. Murdoch.' Jamie paused before adding proudly. 'An' a dinnae need naebody else, I can hurl it masel!' Calum laughed loudly, making Jamie giggle. The two of them got up and made their way to the door.

'I'd better go, Jamie.' said Calum 'Mr. Murdoch widnae be happy finding me in aside his cuddies. I'll see ye later maybe.'

'Ye've no' tae cry them cuddies. Davie says real drayman only hae horses.' Calum laughed, Jamie loved to tell him that. He nodded and waved to Jamie as he left the lamplight and entered the darkness.

Heading towards the Cowgate, Calum rubbed and blew on his hands to warm them. It had been cosy in the stable but it was bitter outside. For a moment he felt strange.

It was almost as if he hadn't gone to sleep. It didn't feel like daytime, it was still so dark. Last night flashed back into his mind again and he shook the memory away. Better not think to about it.

He was glad of the bread and cheese, it set him up for the day. All he needed now was a wee running job to earn him a penny or two. His best bet was the High Street. There was usually someone needing a message. If he were really lucky he'd get a rich gent, new to the city. Sometimes

Calum would clean boots and if the tips were good he could eat for three days on the trot.

He was grinning to himself as he scuttled along, bread and cheese in hand, when suddenly he was knocked sideways. Looking up from the ground he saw a man and a woman, both very drunk. They were laughing and staggering as they walked. They clearly hadn't seen him and hadn't realised they'd knocked him down. Calum glowered at them, his mood completely changed.

'Ye should look where you're goin'' he shouted, picking muck off his precious bread before scoffing it.

'Eh? What?' The woman turned to face Calum, still laughing. 'Aw, look Will...(hic)...we ca'ed the wee fella

o'er. Are ye all right son? Will, gie the wee fella a penny for his trouble, will ye?'

'A penny! For lyin' down! Am I made o' money? Sure, I'll do no such thing, Nellie.'

'Ah go on, Will. You're no' short o' a shillin' the day.' She said tucking her arm in his.

'You're a terrible woman Nellie MacDougal. Here ye go young fella.' He replied, tossing the coin towards Calum without a backward glance. He pocketed it quickly before the man changed his mind.

Something about the man seemed vaguely familiar but Calum couldn't work out what it was. Ah well, thought Calum, a penny closer to a feed and a bed. The couple had moved on slowly and were weaving their way unsteadily towards the corner. They started to sing, loudly and badly. Two seconds later they were out of sight but Calum could hear their song fading.

He set off again for the High street and was almost there when something stopped him in his tracks. He suddenly remembered why the man seemed familiar. It was his voice. He'd heard that same voice the night before. It was the voice of the man with the knife! Suddenly the penny in his pocket felt like a lead weight.

CHAPTER THREE

That afternoon Calum decided to go and see Constable
Fisher. Everybody knew him. He often nipped into the
alehouses in the Grassmarket, the Cowgate and the West
Port. Constable Fisher liked to know what was going on.
Calum was certain he'd want to know about what he'd
seen. He was sure that the men had been up to something
illegal. The barrow had been heavy. Calum's mind was
racing. Maybe the men had robbed one of the big houses.

There was probably silver and gold in the barrow. It could be treasure. Like from a pirate ship with jewels and coins! Maybe Calum would get a reward. He'd be a hero! And rich!

Calum marched determinedly towards the Police Office; Constable Fisher would be on his way out about now. Calum didn't want to miss him and have to traipse around Edinburgh searching all the alehouses for him.

As luck would have it Calum and Constable Fisher met each other on the front step, one going out, one coming in. The police officer was tugging at his collar; it was newly starched and had been choking him all morning. His face was red with irritation. His bushy eyebrows were hunched together and his eyes were dark.

Calum swallowed nervously before speaking up.

'Excuse me sir.'

The constable continued to wrestle with the unforgiving collar, before snapping 'Yes. What do you want? Speak up, boy.'

Calum gulped again, his stomach churning. Perhaps this wasn't such a good idea after all. He took a deep breath. 'I think I've seen some robbers sir.'

Constable Fisher stopped fumbling and looked closely at Calum. 'Do I know you? You been in trouble afore laddie? You look like ye belong in a cell.'

Calum was horrified. He'd come close to being arrested for 'gathering' things but had always managed to escape. 'No sir! I...I...I just wanted to tell ye about the robbers.' Now he was sure this was a *really* bad idea.

'Well, get on with it. I haven't got all day.' The officer grunted, checking the time on his watch chain. Calum blurted out everything; the men sneaking about in

the darkness, the knife and the meeting the next day. He
paused for breath briefly. The constable was standing,
arms folded, listening impatiently. '...so then when the
man spoke I recognised his voice. It was the same voice,
I know it was.' Calum looked up earnestly at the policeman
who was starting to look interested.

'Do you know this man's name?'

'Em, no but I heard the woman call him Will.' Calum
had a flash of inspiration. 'He called her Nellie, Nellie

MacDougal!' Calum was triumphant.

Suddenly Constable Fisher's expression changed. First of all he looked surprised and then he laughed! Calum was baffled. Why was he laughing? Calum was confused and upset. Constable Fisher bent down and ruffled his hair.

'Ye daft wee cratur. Will and Nellie ye say. Ha ha ha. I ken them fine. Will Burke and Nellie MacDougal... they bide in the Hare's lodging house in Tanner's Close. Will's a cobbler laddie, no' a robber! Ha ha ha.' The policeman wiped his nose on his handkerchief and walked off still laughing.

Calum was shaken by his reaction. He couldn't be wrong, could he? No. Calum was convinced – there was something going on and this man Burke was involved. Calum ran after Constable Fisher.

'I'm tellin' the truth sir. It was definitely him. I heard his voice.'

Sighing, the constable turned round slowly.

'An' I'm tellin' you. It wasnae him. Did ye see him rob a hoose?'

'No.'

'Did he stab you wi' a knife?'

'No.'

'Did ye see him stab anither biddy wi' this knife?'

'No.'

'Well, even if ye did see him that nicht we cannae go arrestin' folk for hurlin' a barra.'

'But Constable Fisher...'

'Nae buts. Noo gan awa' afore I belt yer lug. An' stop yer haverin' aboot robbers...Will Burke ...a robber...wait till I tell him...' He walked off shaking his

head and laughing softly to himself. Calum could feel his cheeks burning with anger and shame. He wished he'd never said anything. How could he have been so stupid? Why did no-one ever listen to him? Calum kicked an apple core against the wall. He watched it smash against the stone. One day people *would* listen to him.

CHAPTER FOUR

Some months later Calum was sitting with Jamie in Candlemaker's Row, watching two dogs fighting.

Some men had gathered and were laying bets on the dogfight. Fur and fangs whirled as the two dogs set about each other. One dog was large, black and heavy whilst the other was small, brown and lean. The black dog looked strong but the brown dog was fast. Blood and saliva mixed as the dogs battled. With every bite some men cheered while the others groaned.

Jamie had been hauling beer kegs for Mr Murdoch all morning and had been told to wait for the next delivery. Mrs Murdoch had given him an extra bowl of mutton soup for Calum. They slurped their soup contentedly as they watched the dogs snap and twist in the dust. The men were roaring at the dogs and each other, some were laughing and the mood was good.

Above the noise came a strange sound. Jamie looked at Calum and they stopped slurping for a moment to listen. Some of the men stopped and turned to look too. A young woman was making her way through the crowd, crying and pleading. As she walked she grasped coats and sleeves, tears streaming down her face. Her wailing was high and disturbing. Some men listened for a moment but most shrugged her off and returned their attention to the dogfight.

The woman was quite close to Jamie and Calum now so they could hear what she was saying. 'Have you seen ma pal Mary? Yella hair, blue e'en, she's real bonny…I cannae find her…have ye seen her?' The woman was rambling a little and her words gurgled from her amongst sobs. She zigzagged through the crowd until she came to the two lads sitting on the step. Words tumbled from her mouth like pebbles from a pail.

'Have ye seen Mary? Mary Paterson? She's been missin for days. She widnae go without tellin me. She aye said 'Janet – me an' you are best pals.' Have ye seen her at a'?' She clutched at Jamie's sleeve, hoping he'd seen Mary or spoken to her.

Calum and Jamie shook their heads. Jamie looked as if he was going to cry too. He didn't like it when people were sad, it made him sad. Calum knew he'd have to be quick or Jamie would get very upset.

'Sorry, em… Janet, we havenae seen her. Maybe you should ask at the Police Office?'

'I tried that. They willnae listen tae me.' Janet hung her head. 'They telt me they only had time tae worry about decent folk.'

'Is she a bad lassie then?' asked Jamie, dunking his bread in his bowl. He was feeling a bit better now that Calum was dealing with the greetin' woman.

'No she wisnae a bad lassie!' declared Janet, outraged. 'She jist...did what she did tae mak a wee bawbee. Same as the rest o' us.'

Calum blushed. 'Well, we've no' seen her. Sorry.' He just wanted Janet to go. Her eyes were bloodshot and her face was pale. Tears had left dark lines on her cheeks. In some ways she reminded Calum of his mother. Looking at Janet was like looking at a ghost. The sooner she left, the better. Jamie was happily watching the dogfight again but Calum couldn't get Janet's words out of his head. There were lots of rumours about folk going missing in the city and even more about the dreaded Resurrectionists.

It all made Calum very uneasy. Now it was the summer, Calum was able to sleep outdoors without freezing to death. Some nights though, he wondered if all those stories were true. Sometimes he wondered if he too would be whisked away to the spirit world, or to wherever else the bodies were being taken. He hated being alone, and was glad that Jamie was around.

Jamie had been thrown out of his own home long ago for accidentally pulling down a crockery shelf. His family were very poor and all the dishes had been broken. Jamie was clumsy and his family had had enough. They just couldn't afford to keep Jamie any longer. So out he went. He was as alone as Calum but he didn't seem to worry so much. Jamie trusted everybody. Some days

Calum felt the only person in the world he could trust was Jamie.

He leaned against the sun-warmed stone and smiled as he looked at Jamie, who was wiping up the last of the soup with his bread. He stuck out his tongue and dragged it slowly around his mouth to catch the last drips. Calum laughed despite himself. Jamie looked very funny. He noticed Calum watching and made his eyes cross which was even funnier. Glad of the company, Calum punched him lightly on the arm and they both laughed. Just for a while Calum forgot he was lonely.

CHAPTER FIVE

Whispers were flying up and down the closes and across the landings. Everywhere Calum went, folk were huddled in corners, looking over their shoulders. It was mid October now and the nights were drawing in. Most people were hurrying home; fewer were lingering in the streets. Everyone was afraid. All over the city there was the whisper of disappearances, the whisper of murder! No-one wanted to go out alone at night. It wasn't the dark they feared but what lurked within it. The draymen discussed the rumours, and Calum listened, unseen.

Late one night he was sent on an errand to the West Port and was keen to get it over and done with. He was promised a steaming bowl of porridge if he delivered it quickly. It was well after two in the morning. Calum had asked Jamie to chum him along but he'd not finished his shift yet so, as usual, Calum was on his own.

Hunched against the cold, he stopped to tie his bootlace. As he did so a figure emerged across the road. Something about this figure made Calum stop and crouch very still. In the half-light he could tell it was a man. The

man wore a cap down over his eyes and a scarf up over his mouth. He looked up and down the street then slipped through an alleyway while Calum waited silently. The man returned, this time not alone. The two men rolled a barrel over the cobbles; cu-thump, cu-thump, cu-thump. The noise made Calum's scalp prickle.

'It's no use. We'll have to carry the thing. We'll have the world awake with this racket.' whispered one.

Calum jumped as he recognised the man's voice. It was Burke, the Irishman who'd given him a penny.

'Ah stop your moanin' man. The only racket is you.' replied the other. 'Now shut up before I shut your mouth for you.' A knife blade glinted in the moonlight.

'One of these days, Hare…I swear…' his voice was low and angry.

'You'll what? We've got a fine business here now. If you won't shut up maybe I'll take your Nellie sometime to see the good Doctor Knox.'

The two men stood facing each other across the barrel. Moments passed and then with a sigh Burke grabbed an end of the barrel and they continued on their way.

Calum's mind was racing. Doctor Knox? Where had he heard that name before? Didn't Davie once mention him? Money? What was in the barrel? Where were they going with it? Did he dare follow them? He thought about Constable Fisher; then about his porridge; and regretfully decided that he had to follow the men.

Creeping along behind them was easy. The barrel was clearly heavy because both men were struggling to carry it. They stopped every now and again to catch their breath and straighten their backs. Calum pressed himself into the darkness each time they stopped. They passed no-one. Calum had no choice but to follow. It was the only way to find out what was going on.

Eventually, they arrived at their destination. Calum recognised it as the College of Surgeons. They made their way to a small, side door. The one Calum knew now to be Hare knocked three times on the door. Immediately the door opened and a slab of light from within revealed the

men's faces but only for a moment. A silhouetted figure spoke softly to them and they indicated the barrel. The figure nodded and they all slid the barrel inside. Calum wasn't sure whether to stay or go. He was very cold and didn't want to risk discovery. Perhaps he'd learned enough for one night.

He was just about to leave when the door opened once more. They had been in there no more than three minutes. Both men shook hands with the figure and then left quickly.

Calum stayed still long enough to be certain they were gone then he ran as fast as he could back to the stable to tell Jamie everything. He'd be glad to get back to his porridge and a friendly face.

After Calum had told him what he'd seen Jamie let out a long sigh. He didn't really understand what Calum had said but he was sure Calum was upset, so he was upset. He offered some of his snuff to cheer him up. Calum shook his head and lay down to think for a while. At least he had a bed for the night.

'Aw dinnae be sad Calum. The bad men cannae come here' said Jamie, chewing his lip. 'Can they?'

Calum looked across at Jamie. It wasn't right to worry Jamie.

'No, the bad men cannae come here Jamie. Me an' you will be just fine – dinnae you fash yersel'

The worry on Jamie's face cleared as he lay down on the straw. That was all he needed to hear.

'Nighty night Calum.'

'Night night Jamie.'

It was a very long time before Calum went to sleep. As he stared into the rafters he remembered that Doctor Knox was the man Davie said was using dead bodies in a place called Surgeons Square. He made up his mind, he was going to talk to Constable Fisher again.

CHAPTER SIX

The next morning however, before he could get away to find Constable Fisher, Davie said Calum was needed to replace the other drayman, Alistair. Samson had stepped on his foot and it was broken.

'Yon's an eejit', grumbled Davie, 'if Samson had tramped on his heid we widnae ken the odds.'

Calum laughed and was then so busy working all day that his visit to Constable Fisher was forgotten until he was nearly asleep that night. 'I'll go the morn,' Calum yawned to himself.

'Mmmmm?...Whit did ye say Calum ?' Jamie murmured from under his blanket.

'Nuthin' Jamie. Go back to sleep' Calum yawned again and they were both soon snoring.

The following day there was a frost in the air. Calum and Jamie were glad of the piping hot broth at dinnertime. Jamie was finished first, as usual. He rummaged in his pouch.

'Ach, my days o' the week is near empty. I'll hae tae mind and get some mair.' said Jamie, peering into his little box. He carefully scooped with his little spoon and gave a long sniff then a contented sigh.

'Ye could aye gie it up and there'd be nae mair sneezin'' Calum teased.

'Aw no, I couldnae dae without ma days o' the week.' replied a horrified Jamie, clutching his box to his chest.

Calum had his back to him but eventually Jamie could tell he was laughing. 'You're kiddin' me again, Calum.' he cried and threw a lump of horse manure at the back of Calum's head. It stuck there like a crown of dung. He let out a good natured roar and started chasing Jamie round the yard...

Two weeks later Calum was sweeping out Murdoch's stable yard. Jamie hadn't shown up for work for a week so Mrs. Murdoch had let him help around the stable. They reckoned Jamie must have gone north to the tattie howkin. He'd often talked of going on a trip but nobody thought he'd actually do it.

It was smelly, tiring work at the stable but Calum enjoyed it. He also enjoyed Mrs. Murdoch's baking. She'd promised him a bit of her famous fish pie. Calum's mouth watered at the thought of it. After he'd swept the yard out he'd give the brasses a good polish so she'd give him a lovely big slice. He was still dreaming about the pie when Mrs. Murdoch came rushing out of the scullery, in a panic.

'Have ye heard what they're sayin' aboot Jamie?' Her face was as white as a sheet, her eyes wet with tears.

Calum suddenly felt sick though he wasn't sure why. Mrs. Murdoch was wiping her eyes with her apron and shaking her head in bewilderment. Calum wasn't sure that he wanted to know what 'they' were saying about Jamie. Whatever it was didn't look good.

Mrs. Murdoch sat down heavily on a hay bale to compose herself. She was a large woman and beads of sweat glinted on her skin. Finally she stopped gasping long enough to explain.

'I cannae believe it! The drayman says there's a' sorts o' talk aboot Jamie. They're sayin' he's deid! One o' they medical students was even sayin' that he saw Jamie's body on Doctor Knox's table!'

Hundreds of thoughts jumped about in Calum's head as he tried to work out what was happening. Nothing was making sense and the sick feeling was getting worse. Calum got hotter and hotter and his head began to spin. He felt as if he was being crushed between Cora and Samson. He fell to the ground without a sound.

'Calum...come on son...you're all right. That's it, come on now...open your eyes.'

Bright light made shapes blurred and shadowy. Calum found himself lying down and tried to sit up. The room started to spin again and he fell back against something soft. Gradually his eyes began to adjust and he realised he was inside some sort of bedchamber. 'Where …where am I?' he croaked, his mouth terribly dry. 'What happened to me?'

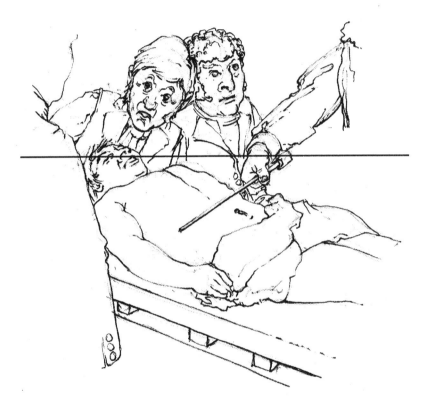

'Shush now…you've had a wee faint. It's me, Mrs. Murdoch. I got Davie to carry you into the backroom. Tak a wee dram tae perk ye up.' She held a thimble of whisky to his lips. He turned away from the smell. Calum's head ached as he tried to remember what had happened.

Then it all came flooding back. His eyes opened wide and he sat straight up.

'JAMIE!' he screamed. Mrs. Murdoch quickly put down the thimble and hugged him tightly.

'Hush now…it's likely only a drunk student's blether. I should never have telt ye. There's aye stories goin' aboot Surgeon's Square. We should pay them nae heed. Jamie's probably been awa' tae get mair snuff for his *days o' the week.*'

This made Calum feel a little better but not much. He sniffed and let Mrs. Murdoch lay him gently down. He was so very tired. She stroked his hand and his hair. His eyes were very heavy. Jamie was probably getting more snuff. Yes, that was it. He was just getting more snuff… Or away at the tattie howkin…

CHAPTER SEVEN

It was Hallowe'en and the streets were busy. Calum had been spending the day helping out at the yard but he decided, at last, that he had to find time to visit the Police-Office. He was very nervous, but he was determined to make Constable Fisher listen to him.

When he got there, the office was busy. He pushed his way to the desk. Many drunks had been arrested and were noisily demanding attention. Constable Fisher looked harassed. Calum wondered if he should just leave but the officer spoke up.

'What do you want? I'm a very busy man.' He hadn't even looked up from his paperwork.

'I think that people are bein' murdered and taken to a man called Doctor Knox.'

The policemen looked up, surprised and then laid down his pen. His face was pale and he licked his lips.

'What do you mean exactly?'

'I think two men called Burke and Hare are killin' folk and takin' their bodies to Surgeon's Square.'

Despite the hustle and bustle around them Calum felt as if he and the policemen were quite alone.

'Follow me.' said the officer, showing him through

to another, quieter room. He pointed to a seat and Calum sat down. 'Tell me everythin', laddie – you're no' the first tae mention these names.'

Calum was sat there for three hours, telling his story, answering questions, telling the same story all over again to another police officer, and answering the same questions all over again. When he finally left, it was dark and he hurried back to the Murdochs. He felt tired and strangely empty. The constable had said he'd be in touch. Now all he could do was wait. When he finally got back he lay down, exhausted, and cried for his best friend Jamie.

In the morning, Calum woke early and splashed cold water from the washstand onto his face. Mrs. Murdoch had managed to persuade her husband to take Calum on. He had Jamie's wee bothy next to the stable block now. It almost felt like home, except that he missed Jamie so much, and also felt funny about taking his bed.

Suddenly, he heard a lot of shouting in the yard. He dried himself off and went to investigate. There was a large crowd in the yard. He couldn't hear what they were saying but he could tell there was a lot of anger. He recognised Davie the drayman, and pushed his way through the crowd to speak to him. The crowd was heading for the alehouse.

'What's goin' on Davie?' asked Calum, looking around him nervously.

' The bobbies have arrested some folk in Tanner's Close. Folk are sayin' that they murdered an auld biddy. Some lodgers reported them and the four o' them are awa' tae the cells.'

Calum felt the sick feeling coming back and prayed he wouldn't faint in front of everyone. Mrs. Murdoch

appeared from the middle of the group and came towards
him. Calum didn't like the look on her face. He could feel
himself getting hot again but fought to stay calm. She
spoke to Davie quietly but Calum could still hear her.

'They say the auld biddy's no' the first. They say
the wicked beggars have been cairtin' folk awa in tea chests
and barrels. For months!'

Calum's legs shook and he realised that he had been
right all along. How he wished he'd been wrong. The

truth was proving unbearable. He leaned against Davie. Mrs. Murdoch nodded and he lifted Calum up and carried him into the bothy.

The next day, Calum heard that the police had found an old lady's body at Doctor Knox's rooms. The Hares and their partners were locked up and were to be charged with her murder.

Calum tried to feel something but he couldn't. He wished that his mother and Jamie were here. Mrs. Murdoch was being very kind but Calum was finding it hard to sleep.

The only thing that seemed to matter was finding out what had happened to Jamie. He thought about him constantly. He tried to listen to rich folk in the park as they read the papers to one another. Slowly little bits of information were revealed. The rest he had to ask.

'What's King's Evidence Davie?' asked Calum, keeping his eyes on Cora's flank as he brushed her. 'I heard men talkin' aboot it at the inn at the West Port.'

Davie had been coiling some rope but stopped before answering.

'Well, it's a special rule in a court. It's when somebody agrees to tell what another person has done - and even if they did it too they won't get punished.'

Calum was stunned.

'So even if Hare m..m..murdered somebody he still won't get hanged?'

'Aye laddie, that's aboot the size o' it.'

'But that's no' fair! He did it tae - I saw him wi' Burke.'

Davie dropped the rope and knelt down beside Calum. 'Aye, it's an awfy business son but sometimes it's better tae get yin than nane.'

Calum pressed his head against Cora's warm, soft skin. He just didn't understand grownups. Davie rubbed his chin and then patted Calum's shoulder. This was such a wicked time but at least the streets would be safer now. Caught like rats…two in the dock, two accusing them. It didn't change how the people of Edinburgh felt. They hated all four of them. Everyone waited for news of the trial.

CHAPTER EIGHT

On Christmas Eve William Burke and Nellie MacDougal
went on trial. Hare and his wife testified against them.
Burke protested that Nellie knew nothing about the murders
and was innocent. He admitted his part; but declared Hare
to be equally guilty. Calum overheard one court officer
tell another that Hare was smirking in his cell and laughing
at the gallows. He was boasting that freedom was a breath
away. Calum sat watching in the public gallery. He could
not take his eyes off Burke. He tried tobut couldn't. Calum

stared so hard his eyes ached. He hated the fact that Hare would not be punished.

Shortly after the trial began, evidence was presented. Calum realised he'd missed much of what the clerk had been saying.

' …items of clothing belonging to the deceased Mary Docherty have been confirmed as such by the deceased's daughter. In addition may I present Exhibit C: one pair of boy's breeches, owner unknown.' There was a gasp and some sobs from the crowded gallery.

Mrs. Murdoch had forbidden Calum to attend the trial but he had been unable to stay away. Something inside

him made him go. He sat, a very small figure, amongst muttering angry citizens hoping for justice and safety on the streets.

Finally the moment came that Calum had dreaded. One of the court officers held up a little snuffbox with seven holes and a little copper spoon to match. Even from a distance Calum knew they were Jamie's. The clerk continued.

'Exhibit D: one small, copper snuffbox with seven holes in the lid. Exhibit E: one small, copper spoon. Both articles alleged to belong to one James Wilson, known in some parts as Daft Jamie...'

When Calum saw them he thought his heart would break. Poor, poor Jamie – always so trusting. Calum got up to go. He didn't need to hear any more. The sick feeling was so strong he had to slide his hand along the wall to stay standing. He left the building and slowly walked home, sobbing. He wasn't in court to hear the jury reaching a decision.

Old Mary Docherty had been been suffocated. Burke had held her mouth closed and pinched her nostrils so she couldn't breathe. Hare had held her down so she couldn't fight back. All the victims had died this way. Burke admitted to at least ten murders, including Jamie's, saying;

'We had often said we may as well be hung for a sheep as a lamb,'

The case against Nellie MacDougal was found Not Proven; but William Burke was found guilty of murder, and sentenced to death. The judge decided that, because of the horrid nature of the crimes, Burke must not simply be hanged, but that his body was to be dissected, just like those of his victims, and then put on public display.

A date was set and on January 28th 1829 William Burke was hanged. Twenty five thousand people gathered to watch and Calum was one of them. He had never seen so many people. It felt as if the whole world had come to see Burke swing.

Surrounded by a huge angry mob Calum felt as if he was underwater. None of this felt real to him. He wasn't sure about anything any more. Why did Hare go unpunished? What about Doctor Knox? Why Jamie? Men and woman were screaming abuse at Burke as he stood at the gallows. They cheered as his body dropped. Calum felt nothing but sadness and a longing for an end to his nightmares. Mrs. Murdoch put her arm around his shoulders and held him tight against her.

From that day on, Nellie MacDougal was hounded wherever she went. No-one believed she was innocent. The Hares split up and went their separate ways. The stain of their guilt hung over them like a bad smell. No-one would stay in their boarding house. Hare even tried to make money out of his story - but no-one would pay him for it, and he died penniless. His wife had disappeared long before. Rumour said that she died a miserable death.

Calum sat on his bed and got ready to blow out his candle. Mrs. Murdoch had said he could stay at the yard forever, if he wanted. He was warm, well fed and safe. Maybe now that it was all over he might sleep properly again. He gazed at the little flame thoughtfully, 'Nighty night, Jamie' he whispered. 'Sleep well.'

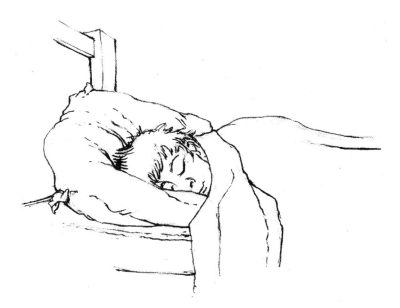

GLOSSARY

AFORE before

AULD BIDDY old person

AULD REEKIE Edinburgh

AWFY awful

BAWBEE penny

BIDE stay

BLETHER chat

CA'ED O'ER knocked over

CANNAE cannot

CLOSES hallways in tenements

CRATUR creature

CUDDIES horses

DINNAE do not

DRAYMAN delivers barrels by horse and cart

EEJIT idiot

HAVERIN' speaking nonsense

HEID head

LANDINGS upstairs levels of tenements

LUG ear

Reader's Notes

This story is a fictional account based on real life events leading to the execution of William Burke. The characters of Calum, Constable Fisher and Mrs. Murdoch are fictional.

In the 1820s medical research was high profile and subjects for study were in high demand. Although the majority of bodies came to the universities by legal means the prospect of easy money lead to an increase in grave robbing.

Families recently bereaved were anxious to protect their loved ones and paid night watchmen to prevent criminals stealing bodies under the cover of darkness. These criminals came to be known as Resurrectionists in a direct reference to the Christian belief of rising from the dead.

Contrary to popular belief Burke and Hare did not participate in grave robbing. Their initial involvement in medical research came about by chance when two lodgers died, leaving outstanding rent. Having no relatives to miss them Burke and Hare decided to recoup their lost rental income by selling the bodies for medical research. They soon realised the potential and when no further bodies came their way through natural causes they turned to murder.

Although there was great scandal during and after the case, Dr Knox was never charged with any offence. The extent of his involvement has never been fully clarified.

Teachers reading this may wish to note that this book dovetails with the Scottish curriculum in

- Environmental Studies
- Personal and Social Health Education
- Philosophy
- Language

Further information on Rooshie-Doo books, and suggestions for their use in schools, can be found on the publisher's website at www.galluspublications.com

If you have enjoyed this book, you may also enjoy…

Threat! A story of Mary Slessor by Karen Doherty

Accused! A story of Beatrix Laing by Susan Greig

Cannibals! A story of Sawney Bean by Helen Welsh

Reformed! A story of Jenny Geddes by Helen Welsh